To Juniper, Long John
and Bronte-saurus

First published 2015 by Walker Books Ltd
87 Vauxhall Walk, London SE11 5HJ

1 2 3 4 5 6 7 8 9 10

© 2015 George O'Connor

This book has been typeset in Aunt Mildred

Printed in China

British Library Cataloguing in Publication Data:
a catalogue record for this book is available from the British Library

ISBN 978-1-4063-6034-9

www.walker.co.uk

WALKER BOOKS
AND SUBSIDIARIES
LONDON · BOSTON · SYDNEY · AUCKLAND

IF I HAD A TRICERATOPS

George O'Connor

If I had a triceratops,
I'd be sure to take good care of her.
Owning a triceratops is a lot of work.

I would give her a house of her own
in the back garden with lots of room
to run around.

If I had a triceratops,

I would take her for lots and lots of walks.

(I'd make sure I cleaned up after her, of course.)

Going for walks would give my
triceratops a great chance
to make new friends.

(And me too, I guess.)

Playing fetch would be another
excellent way for her to get exercise.

If I had a triceratops,
I'd train her well and
teach her tricks,
like ...

sit up,

roll over

and play dead.

High five!

I bet my triceratops would like to dig holes.

If she found any large bones,
I wouldn't let her chew on them.

She could choke.
(And besides, they might
belong to a relative of hers.)

When she got dirty, I'd give her a bath.

If I had a triceratops, she would protect my home from burglars. (And maybe even the occasional T-Rex.)

And if sometimes she got into trouble —
like for eating my homework ...

or chasing the neighbour's car — well ...

it would all be worth it

when she ran out to greet me

at the end of the day.

There's my girl!

If I had a triceratops,
I would be the luckiest kid in the world.